ROBO FORCE
AND THE
GIANT ROBOT

SPECIAL ROBO FORCE INSTRUCTIONS
FOR THE READER OF THIS BOOK:

Read this book carefully. When you are asked to help the Robo Force, you must solve a puzzle. You will be given two choices. Pick the one that you think is right. Then turn to the page that goes with your choice. Choose wisely, Robo Force warrior!

ROBO FORCE AND THE GIANT ROBOT

By Seth McEvoy • Illustrated by Penalva

These are the members of the Robo Force team:

S.O.T.A., the Creator

Maxx Steele, the Leader

Wrecker, the Demolisher

Coptor, the Enforcer

Blazer, the Ignitor

Sentinel, the Protector

RANDOM HOUSE 🏠 NEW YORK

BLAZER, COPTOR, DRED CRAWLER, FORTRESS OF STEELE, HUN-DRED, ROBO FORCE, SENTINEL, S.O.T.A., MAXX STEELE, NAZGAR, VULGAR, and WRECKER are trademarks of CBS Inc. and are used under license.

Wrecker and S.O.T.A., two members of the Robo Force, are repairing a solar power collector near the farming district of the planet Zeton.

"Move it left three robo-inches," says S.O.T.A.

"But I just moved it three robo-inches to the right!" growls Wrecker. "Make up your mind, jerk-circuits! My favorite holo-TV program starts in an hour."

4

Suddenly the power collector begins to shake! "What's happening?" shouts Wrecker.

"It's a Zeton-quake!" yells S.O.T.A. "Look out!"

The heavy girders snap like twigs. They crash down onto S.O.T.A. and Wrecker.

Turn to page 6.

5

"Are you okay?" asks Wrecker as he climbs out from under the power collector.

"My circuits report no damage," answers S.O.T.A. "However, that was definitely *not* a Zeton-quake. My sonar tells me that it was caused by unknown forces."

Wrecker pulls S.O.T.A. free with his mighty grapplers. "So what was it?"

The ground shakes again! Looking up, S.O.T.A. and Wrecker see a giant robot coming toward them.

"Look at that metal monstrosity!" shouts S.O.T.A. "It's twenty times larger than we are."

"I have a bad feeling in my rivets about this," mutters Wrecker.

Turn to page 8.

S.O.T.A. and Wrecker climb to the top of the broken power collector to get a better look at the approaching giant robot.

"Hey, I'd recognize that creep anywhere," says Wrecker.

S.O.T.A. uses his telescopic vision. "It's the evil robot Vulgar," he says. "How did he get so big?"

"Maybe by eating a good breakfast of Robo Crunchies every morning," answers Wrecker. "Here he comes!"

Turn to page 10.

The giant-size Vulgar smashes his way through the rest of the power collector!

The two members of the Robo Force fly out of the way. "That was close!" says S.O.T.A.

"We'd better call for help," Wrecker says. "He'll destroy everything in sight if we don't stop him."

S.O.T.A. flies after the giant robot. "There's no time. Vulgar will destroy half the planet's food supply before the rest of the Robo Force can get here. It's up to us."

Turn to page 12.

"How can we stop Vulgar?" asks Wrecker. "Even my laser drill can't cut through something that big!"

"If we can get inside his body, we can shut down his control center," answers S.O.T.A.

"How about this hatch here? I've never seen one like it on a robot before," Wrecker says.

"Watch out! It's booby-trapped," warns S.O.T.A. Then he uses his radar to study the hatch.

S.O.T.A's computer brain senses that *one* of the gears on the hatch is not the same as any other. "If we pull off the odd gear, we can get the hatch open safely," he says. "It's one of these two gears, but I'm not sure which one."

Help the Robo Force! Which gear is the odd one?

If you think it is gear A, tell Wrecker to yank it off. Then turn to page 14.

If you think it is gear B, tell Wrecker to yank it off. Then turn to page 16.

Hurry! Vulgar will reach the crops in a few more minutes!

The hatch explodes! S.O.T.A. and Wrecker are blasted through the air. They land in the mud!

"I think we picked the wrong gear," says Wrecker as he cleans himself off.

"We'll try again!" says S.O.T.A. "The Robo Force never gives up!"

The two robots fly back to the giant Vulgar.

Turn to page 16.

Wrecker yanks the correct gear off the hatch. It opens safely.
"Quick!" whispers S.O.T.A. "Get in before Vulgar notices."
The two Robo Force robots fly through the hatch. "Is this what
I look like inside?" asks Wrecker.

"Yes, but with much less rust! Now, be quiet. I'm going to use this giant information plug to get into Vulgar's computer data bank."

The giant plug is as big as S.O.T.A.'s body, but he can still use it by sticking his arm in the socket. After a few moments S.O.T.A. reports, "I've got it!"

"What—Robo-measles? I've been waiting long enough. Can't we just start smashing?" says Wrecker impatiently.

S.O.T.A. projects a laser blueprint of Vulgar's robot body on the wall. "These blueprints will show us the quickest way to Vulgar's power center! Let's go."

Turn to page 18.

Suddenly Wrecker's path is blocked by a giant creature! "What is it?" he shouts. "Those metal teeth look like they can bite a robot in half!"

"It's a Romite!" answers S.O.T.A. "Whatever made Vulgar so big made his Romites big too."

"Ugh! Only robots who don't take weekly oil baths have Romites," says Wrecker. "Look out! It's coming after us!"

"Run!"

Turn to page 20.

More Romites block the path. "We'll have to fight," says S.O.T.A.

Wrecker turns on his atomic jackhammer. "Taste this, Romites!" he shouts.

While Wrecker attacks the Romites in front, S.O.T.A. leads the rest down a corridor in Vulgar's body to a place where several big wires cross.

"Just what I wanted!" S.O.T.A. says. He grabs the wires and pulls them apart.

Deadly electric sparks fly from the wires!

Holding the wires carefully, S.O.T.A. shocks the Romites until every one of them is stunned.

Turn to page 22.

Wrecker leads the way upward to Vulgar's power center. S.O.T.A. follows, keeping an alert watch for Romites.

The two robots come to a huge pool of grease. "Vulgar sure could use a good cleaning!" says Wrecker as he wades through the treacherous grease. "One slip and I might never get out!"

"Watch out for those electrodes!" shouts S.O.T.A. a moment later. "If you touch them your rivets will pop off!"

As the two robots climb higher, they hear a loud grinding noise. "My extended hearing tells me we're getting close to Vulgar's shoulder gears," warns S.O.T.A.

"Nothing to it!" says Wrecker bravely. He flies through the whirling gears without a scratch.

S.O.T.A. follows. "We're almost there!"

Turn to page 24.

23

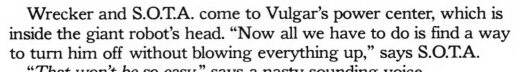

Wrecker and S.O.T.A. come to Vulgar's power center, which is inside the giant robot's head. "Now all we have to do is find a way to turn him off without blowing everything up," says S.O.T.A.

"*That won't be so easy,*" says a nasty-sounding voice.

The two robots turn around and see a video screen above the control center. On the screen is Hun-Dred, Nazgar's cruelest robot!

24

"When I used my enlarging ray to make Vulgar into a giant," he says, "I also fixed his control center so that if anybody tried to turn him off, they would blow themselves up."

"We don't care!" shouts Wrecker defiantly. "The Robo Force isn't afraid of an explosion or two!"

Hun-Dred laughs. "But this explosion will destroy Zeton's farmlands," he brags. "What do you think of that?"

Turn to page 26.

S.O.T.A. quickly opens the control center.
Inside are many wires of different colors.

"Get out of there, you mechanical
meathead!" yells Hun-Dred.
"You'll just blow yourself up!"

"Maybe not," says S.O.T.A.
as he begins to study the wires.

"They don't call me
State Of The Art for nothing."

26

Soon he finishes analyzing the wiring of the control center. "We can stop Vulgar if we cut all the red wires," he tells Wrecker. "Use your laser drill, but be careful not to use it more often than you need to. Cut each red wire once."

Help the Robo Force! The wires are tangled. How many separate red wires are there?

If you see seven separate red wires, tell Wrecker to fire seven times. Then turn to page 28.

If you see six separate red wires, tell Wrecker to fire six times. Then turn to page 30.

Wrecker fires his laser drill seven times. All the red wires are cut! Vulgar's giant robot body crashes to the ground. His motors stop moving. Vulgar's power center is dark and silent. "I did it!" shouts Wrecker. "Zeton is saved!"

"But we're not!" says S.O.T.A. "My microscopic scanners report that Vulgar's body is starting to shrink. If we don't get out in time, we'll be squeezed into robo-jelly!"

"But it's too dark! How will we find our way out?"

"Hang on to me. My infrared vision will guide us," says S.O.T.A. "Hurry!"

Turn to page 32.

Wrecker fires his laser drill six times. The two robots wait. Vulgar is still moving!

Suddenly a red ray shoots out of the power center. "We're getting larger!" shouts S.O.T.A. "We'll be crushed against Vulgar's inner walls!"

Wrecker yells, "I must have missed one of those red wires." He fires again and blasts the last red wire.

"Whew!" he says. "That was close!" The two robots shrink back to their normal size. "We did it! Zeton is safe!"

"But we're not!" yells S.O.T.A. "Now *Vulgar* is shrinking! If we don't get out of here, we'll be mashed robo-potatoes!"

Turn to page 32.

Wrecker and S.O.T.A. fly through the corridors of Vulgar's robot body. They come to the hatch and Wrecker pops out.

"I'm stuck!" shouts S.O.T.A.

Wrecker uses his mighty strength to pull S.O.T.A. through the hatch—just in time.

Vulgar is normal size again. But before they can take him back to the Fortress of Steele, a Dred Crawler swoops down from the sky. Hun-Dred is at the controls! He snatches Vulgar away from S.O.T.A. and Wrecker.

"I'll destroy you tin-plated toads another day," he says as he flies away.

"Won't you ever learn?" shouts Wrecker. "Even a giant robot can't beat the Robo Force!"